DISNEY PRINCESS

Sleeping Beauty

PaRRagon

Bath · New York · Singapore · Hong Kong · Cologne · Delhi · Melbourne

Narrator, King Stefan and King Hubert Bob Holt
Maleficent and Merryweather Linda Gary

Once Upon a Dream
Performed by Mary Costa, Bill Shirley and Chorus
Music and Lyrics by Sammy Fain and Jack Lawrence
© 1952 Walt Disney Music Company (ASCAP). © renewed. All rights
reserved. International © renewed.
℗ 1959 Walt Disney Records

This edition published by Parragon in 2010

Parragon
Queen Street House
4 Queen Street
Bath BA1 1HE, UK

℗ 2010 Walt Disney Records © Disney
Copyright © 2010 Disney Enterprises, Inc.

All rights reserved. No part of this publication may be reproduced,
stored in a retrieval system or transmitted, in any form or by any
means, electronic, mechanical, photocopying, recording or
otherwise, without the prior permission of the copyright holder.

ISBN 978-1-4454-4157-3

Printed in China

This is the story of Sleeping
Beauty. You can read along with
me in your book. You will know it
is time to turn the page when you
hear the chimes ring like this...

Let's begin now:

In a far away land, long ago, lived King Stefan and his fair queen. One day a daughter was born and they called her Aurora. They named her after the dawn, for she filled their lives with sunshine.

From near and far the people came, bringing their
gifts, to celebrate the royal birth.

The most honoured guests were the three good
fairies: Fauna, Flora and Merryweather. Each could
give the child a single gift. Flora blessed the child
with beauty. Fauna gave the gift of song, that she
might sing like a nightingale.

Little Merryweather was about to give her gift when suddenly there was a roar of thunder and a gust of wind. A blinding flash of light filled the great hall, and before them stood the evil Maleficent. "Well, King Stefan. I was quite upset at not receiving an invitation. I, too, have a gift to bestow on the child.

"The princess shall indeed grow in grace and beauty. But before the sun sets on her sixteenth birthday, she shall prick her finger on the spindle of a spinning wheel, and die!"

"Oh, no!" The cry rose from every heart. But before anyone could seize Maleficent and make her take back her evil curse, she had vanished in a flash of flame. What a terrible situation! But there was hope. Merryweather still had her gift to give. "Your Majesties, I cannot undo this wicked curse, but I can help."

Merryweather waved her magic wand over the cradle.

"Sweet Princess, if all this should come to pass, not in death, but just in sleep, the fateful prophecy you will keep. And from this slumber you shall awake, when true love's kiss the spell shall break."

But King Stefan was still fearful for his daughter's life.

"This does not take away the evil threat. We must take action! Let every spindle and spinning wheel in the country be burned!"

That night, the countryside was aglow with the light of burning spinning wheels.

Meanwhile, the three good fairies were trying to think of a better plan. Merryweather told the others, "A bonfire won't stop Maleficent. There must be some way we can protect Aurora from that wicked old witch! I know. Let us raise the Princess in a secret hiding place. We will keep her safe until her sixteenth birthday." Sadly, the King and Queen agreed.

Disguised as simple peasant women, the three good fairies took the young Princess to a tiny cottage deep in the woods.

They called her Briar Rose instead of Aurora, and never told her she was a Princess. So for sixteen years, the whereabouts of Aurora remained a mystery.

On her sixteenth birthday, Briar Rose was picking berries, when she chanced to meet a handsome young man riding in the forest. He was very kind. She was rather shy.

She was not supposed to speak with strangers, but Briar Rose felt as if she knew him, for she had often dreamed of meeting someone so charming.

She asked him to come to the cottage that evening and meet her family. Then Briar Rose rushed home to tell Flora, Fauna and Merryweather her happy news.

She was falling in love.

When Briar Rose told the fairy godmothers about her true love, they grew sad. "Since it's your sixteenth birthday, we must tell you the truth now. You are really the Princess Aurora. Your marriage to Prince Philip will take place this very evening in your father's castle. You can never see your handsome stranger again." Briar Rose burst into tears.

Meanwhile, the young stranger rode off to tell his father that he had just met the girl of his dreams. Actually, the young man was Prince Philip. When he told his father King Hubert about Briar Rose, the King became very upset.

"What? You've fallen in love with some peasant girl? I won't have it! I promised my neighbour, King Stefan that you would marry his daughter Aurora! You're a Prince! And you're going to marry a Princess!"

But Philip's mind was made up. Off he rode to the cottage in the woods to meet his true love, Briar Rose.

But she was not there. The three good fairies had carefully escorted her to King Stefan's castle. The poor Princess should have been happy, but all she could think of was her lost love.

Merryweather led her up to her room.

"Cheer up, dear. You can't meet your father looking so glum. We'll leave you alone for a few moments to dry your tears."

While the good fairies waited outside, a mysterious
voice began calling to the sad Princess. "Aurora. Aurora."
In a trance she followed the haunting sound up a winding
stairway to the top of the tower.

Off in the distance Merryweather heard the evil chant.

"Listen! It's Maleficent!" The fairies rushed through the palace corridors searching for the Princess. "Rose! Rose! Don't touch anything!"

But Maleficent's curse was far too powerful. The evil fairy called out from the shadows. "Touch the spindle. Touch it, I say!" As if in a dream, Aurora stretched out her hand to touch the shining spindle.

The fairies finally found Maleficent, but alas, it was too late.
"You poor simple fools. Thinking you could defeat me. Me,
mistress of all evil! Well, here's your precious Princess."

Maleficent pulled back her long cape to reveal the beautiful
Aurora lying in a deep sleep.

Maleficent disappeared in a blaze of light. Her curse was
complete. Now only true love's kiss could save Aurora.

Merryweather knew they must do something. "No one must ever know of this wicked deed. We'll put everyone to sleep until Rose awakens."

As the fairies cast their spell over the castle, they heard King Hubert say, "My son Philip has lost his head. He fell in love with some girl named Briar Rose."

Flora realized that the young stranger Rose had met in the forest was really Prince Philip.

But miles away, Maleficent was plotting. "Prince Philip is the only person who can break my evil curse. I must find him at once." She and her demon army captured Philip and locked him in a deep dungeon.

But the good fairies flew to Philip's rescue and freed him. They armed him with a magic sword and led him to the sleeping Princess.

Maleficent was furious when she found that the Prince had escaped. Determined to stop him, she turned herself into a fiery dragon. But her evil could not overcome Philip's magic sword and his true love. Maleficent was destroyed.

With the help of the three fairies, Prince Philip found the tiny tower room where his sleeping beauty lay.

There, dreaming of her true love, was the Princess Aurora – the very same girl he had fallen in love with.

He gave her a kiss. She opened her eyes and smiled. Maleficent's spell was broken.

Soon the whole castle was awake and the joyous wedding celebration began.

And so, the sleeping beauty and her own true love were married and lived happily ever after.